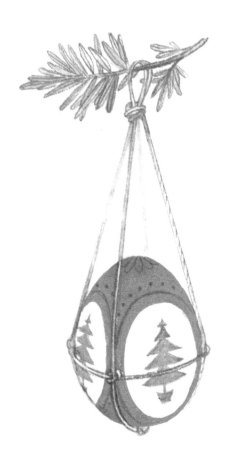

The Christmas Party
Adrienne Adams

Aladdin Books
Macmillan Publishing Company   New York
Maxwell Macmillan Canada   Toronto
Maxwell Macmillan International
New York   Oxford   Singapore   Sydney

Second Aladdin Books edition 1992
First Aladdin Books edition 1982
Copyright © 1978 by Adrienne Adams

Aladdin Books   Maxwell Macmillan Canada, Inc.
Macmillan Publishing Company   1200 Eglinton Avenue East
866 Third Avenue   Suite 200
New York, NY 10022   Don Mills, Ontario M3C 3N1

Macmillan Publishing Company is part of the Maxwell Communication
Group of Companies.

Printed in the United States of America
10 9 8 7 6 5 4 3 2 1
A hardcover edition of *The Christmas Party* is available from Charles
Scribner's Sons Books for Young Readers, Macmillan Publishing Company.

Library of Congress Cataloging-in-Publication Data
Adams, Adrienne.
The Christmas party / by Adrienne Adams.
p.   cm.
Reprint. Originally published: New York: Scribner's, © 1978.
Summary: Orson Abbott helps a group of younger rabbits organize a
surprise Christmas party for their parents.
ISBN 0-689-71630-3
[1. Rabbits—Fiction. 2. Christmas—Fiction.]   I. Title
PZ7.A194Ch   1992   91-42159
[E]—dc20

For Galen Martinez

Even before Christmas, the Abbotts were busy getting ready for Easter.

Everyone knew young Orson Abbott and his parents. They were the Easter egg artists.

Orson felt like a grown-up, even though he wasn't. And he really loved being an artist. He could make every egg different from all the others, if he wished.

Orson heard a tapping at the window and looked up. The studio window was filled with young rabbits.

"I wish those kids would leave me alone," Orson said. "Can't they see I have work to do?" He refused to pay any attention to them, and finally they went away.

At bedtime, Orson bundled up to go out.

His mother said, "It's cold out there, the coldest night yet. Why don't you sleep in here tonight?"

"But I'm cozy in my tree house," Orson said. "And it's all mine. No one can get up there unless I let him."

He went outside and across the yard to a very tall tree. There he pulled himself up to his tree house in the bucket elevator he had made.

When he looked out the next morning, he found the
bunch of little rabbits chattering under his tree.

"Hi, Snopsy," Orson said to the biggest bunny. "What's
up?"

"You are!" Snopsy shouted. "Will you let me come up
and see your house? Please?"

"Why should I?" Orson asked.

"My father says I can build *me* a tree house, but how
can I if you won't let me see how you did it?"

"We-ell — okay," Orson said. "Just this once."

Of course, the first thing he knew, he was hauling up not only Snopsy, but *everybody*. His pad was jammed.

"What a mob!" he cried. "Why are all you little kids hanging around together anyway?"

"Well," said a small rabbit, taking a deep breath. "We want to have a Christmas party as a surprise for our parents, and we wanted to ask if you would help us."

Orson was stunned. "You want to *give* a party? How can you do that?"

"We can if you help us," said Snopsy. "How about here at your place — not in the tree house, but down in the yard maybe?"

"Oh no you don't! That's too much work," said Orson.

"But we'll do it all!" yelled the little rabbits.

Orson felt sure they wouldn't, but he knew he was trapped.

"We-ell, all right," he said.

When Orson went in the house for breakfast he told his parents what he had done. "How can I get out of it?" he asked.

"Why do you want to get out of it?" asked his father.

"It will be a lot of work. You know those kids won't do much. I'll be doing it all."

"But, Orson," said his mother. "Didn't you promise?"

"I think it sounds like fun," said Father Abbott. "Let's go find a Christmas tree."

When Orson saw his father and mother setting out across the snow with an axe, he followed reluctantly.

They found the perfect Christmas tree and cut it down. But it was too heavy for the three of them to take home.

"This looks like a good job for that bunch of kids," Orson said. "There are enough of them to do it I'm sure."

And there were. They did the whole job by themselves
—pushing, shoving, pulling, hauling the tree on their sleds,
and yelling like a pack of coyotes. It was a pretty big pack by
now.

Orson and his father made a base for the tree that could be turned. That way, they could decorate the whole tree from Orson's elevator.

Finally the tree was up. Orson looked at it proudly.

"I have a terrific idea," he said. "Why don't we decorate it with eggs? We certainly have enough of them."

"Eggs?" Snopsy yelled. "*Easter* eggs? Hey, that's a neat idea!"

The next day everybody was helping with the tree dec-
orations. Mother Abbott popped popcorn, and the little ones
strung yards and yards of it on thread.

Father and Orson chose the Easter eggs that seemed

best for Christmas, and Orson painted some special ones just for the occasion.

Then everybody went outside to decorate the tree. As they worked, big white snowflakes began to fall.

It was the day before Christmas.

"Okay, let's go inside now and get the presents ready," said Orson. "No muddy shoes in the house — just leave 'em at the door."

Mother Abbott smiled gratefully at her son.

When all of the little rabbits were settled and working Orson said, "Hey, Mom, how about a Santa suit?"

"He already has one," his mother said.

"He? Who?"

"Your father."

"Father?" Orson yelled as if he had been shot. "I'm Santa."

"Oh," Mother Abbott said. "Pleased to meet you."

"Gee, Mom, can't you make me a suit out of something?"

"Of course I can. Come here and let me measure you — you *grow* so!"

Finally everything was almost ready. In the middle of his Santa suit fitting, Orson suddenly thought of something he had to take care of outside. Mother Abbott trailed him out of the house with pins in her mouth and a sleeve in her hands.

"When he gets started," she said later to Father Abbott, "he's a ball of fire."

With Orson in charge, everything was ready by sunset.

"This is it — Christmas Eve," Orson said. "I'm really proud of you kids. Now, everybody scamper home and talk your folks into a moonlight sled ride, whether they like it or not."

Soon after dark, the Abbotts saw the sleds in the moonlight streaking down all the hills around.

By the time the guests arrived, Orson was hiding in his pad, all dressed up in his special Santa suit.

At exactly the right moment Orson turned on a switch. The spotlights flooded the Christmas tree.

The young rabbits all screamed, "Surprise! MERRY CHRISTMAS!"

Their parents almost fell over backwards.

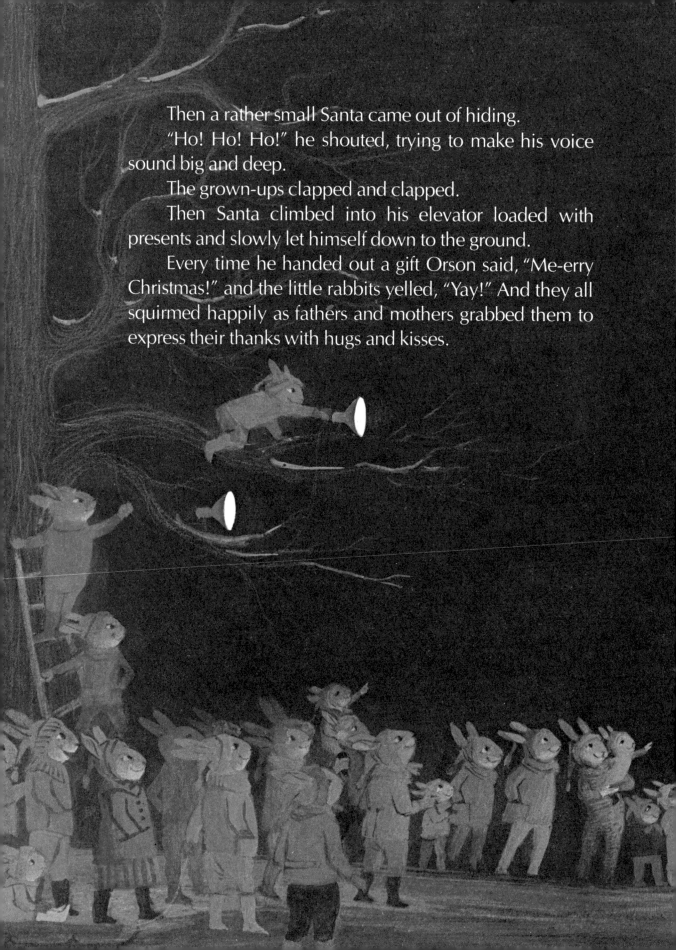

Then a rather small Santa came out of hiding.

"Ho! Ho! Ho!" he shouted, trying to make his voice sound big and deep.

The grown-ups clapped and clapped.

Then Santa climbed into his elevator loaded with presents and slowly let himself down to the ground.

Every time he handed out a gift Orson said, "Me-erry Christmas!" and the little rabbits yelled, "Yay!" And they all squirmed happily as fathers and mothers grabbed them to express their thanks with hugs and kisses.

Then the youngsters built up the fire and roasted their most favorite food — hot dogs!

When it was all over, Snopsy's father said, "It was the best party *ever*." And all of the other parents shouted, "Yay!"

The little rabbits, tired as they were, grinned broadly at each other. Orson patted them proudly on their backs as they left for home.

It was a pretty sight as the guests climbed the hills to their homes. Many of the grown-ups were pulling the exhausted children on the sleds.

The Abbotts sighed happily.

"Let's go to bed," Mother Abbott said, "and leave the mess until tomorrow."

"Don't worry about the mess," Orson said, yawning. "Those are good kids. They'll be back early tomorrow to clean up I'm sure." Before he could say another word he was asleep in his chair.

Mother Abbott removed the sleeping Santa's beard.

"He's becoming very grown-up," she said softly to Father Abbott.

"Yes," Father Abbott replied. "He certainly made it a Merry Christmas for that bunch of little kids."

"And for us, too," said Mother Abbott. "Goodnight, dear, and Merry Christmas."

"Merry Christmas."